STOⱯ

FRIENDS
OF ACPL

W9-CIA-592

4/99

With thanks to, and in celebration of,
special friends in far off places.
J.B. & T.B.

First published in Great Britain in 1997
by Levinson Books Ltd.
This edition published by David & Charles Children's Books,
Winchester House, 259-269 Old Marylebone Road, London NW1 5XJ

10 9 8 7 6 5 4 3 2

Text copyright © Jemma Beeke 1997
Illustrations copyright © Tiphanie Beeke 1997

The right of Jemma Beeke and Tiphanie Beeke to be identified
as the author and illustrator of this work has been asserted by them
in accordance with the Copyright Designs and Patents Act 1988.

ISBN 1 899607 66 8 hardback
ISBN 1 86233 037 9 paperback

Printed in Belgium.

the Brand New Creature

David&Charles
Children's Books

One morning, I decided to find a crocodile. I was bored with the chicken that scratched and strutted about in the yard. I was bored, too, with the lazy cat that stretched itself out and stayed asleep all day.

I had never seen
a crocodile, nor any
other wild creature, but I knew
that a crocodile would be much more
fun to play with than a chicken or a cat.

The sun was shining brightly when I left the

The dusty ground was

I walked and walked

garden and set out on my search.

baked hard and hot.

for many miles before I met anything at all.

Then I saw
a creature with
a long, scaly body
of beautiful colours.

It was wrapped around and
about the branches of a tree.
'Excuse me, but are you a
crocodile?' I asked politely.

The creature
stared at me
and whispered softly,
'No, for a crocodile
cannot slither and slide
as smoothly as I can.'

'Then I am sorry to have
troubled you,' I said.

Presently, I came to four slender
patchy brown and cream legs. I looked up
and saw that these tall, tall legs belonged to
a creature with a very long neck.

It bowed its head to listen as I asked politely,
'Excuse me, but are you a crocodile?'

The creature blinked its long lashes slowly,
'No. A crocodile is not nearly as tall as I am,
and it does not have such a pretty pattern.'
'Then I am sorry to have troubled you,' I said.

Next I met a proud, golden creature
with a thick brown mane all about its face.
'Excuse me, but are you a crocodile?'
I asked politely.

The creature looked offended and
gave a low growl. 'Certainly not,'
it roared. 'I am far more handsome than
a crocodile and far more important.'
'Then I am sorry to have troubled you,' I said.

The next wild creature I met was
covered with black and white feathers.
Its body seemed too big for its gangly pink legs.
'Excuse me, but are *you* a crocodile?'
I asked politely.

'Me? A crocodile? Oh no, no, no, no, no!' it gasped, flapping its wings. 'How could I possibly be a crocodile with my fine feathers and lovely legs? Silly child!'

'Then I am sorry to have troubled you,' I said.

I kept walking until I met another creature. I had to try hard not to laugh out loud because this was the oddest-looking creature I had seen all day. It had such a funny-shaped head and huge snout.

'Excuse me, but are *you* a crocodile?' I asked.

The creature looked at me, and sadly grunted,
'No. A crocodile is not as ugly as I am.'
'Then I am sorry to have troubled you,' I said.

After a while I saw an enormous creature with crinkly grey skin, and (although I wouldn't say so to its face) a *very* long nose. 'Excuse me, but are you a crocodile?' I asked politely.

The creature gave a great snort.
'What? Me? A crocodile?
Certainly not!' it trumpeted.
'I am much stronger than a
crocodile, and far more noble.'
'Then I am sorry to have
troubled you,' I said.

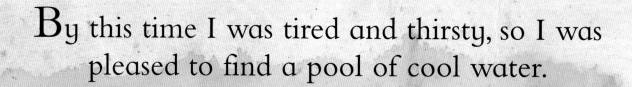

By this time I was tired and thirsty, so I was pleased to find a pool of cool water.

As I drank, I thought about all the wild creatures I had seen that day. Each one of them was different from the chicken and the cat, but none of them was a crocodile.

As the sun was beginning to go down,
I got up sadly to begin my long,
lonely walk home.

But just then I saw a shiny white egg lying
by itself in the red dust. I crouched down to
look at it more closely, and then . . .

CCCRRRA

ACCCKKK

The egg broke apart into two halves
and out crawled a brand new creature.

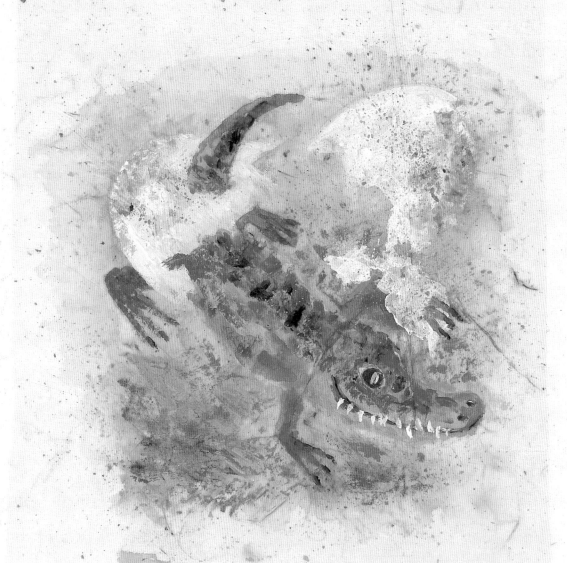

Its brand new body was
green and bumpy, and its
brand new face had a long, flat snout.
It had four brand new feet, and one
long, pointed brand new tail.
It smiled its brand new smile at me.

'I don't suppose you know what
a crocodile looks like,' I said quite
rudely (because by now I felt
tired and cross).

The brand new creature laughed its brand new
laugh, and said in its brand new voice,
'No, I do not know. I am a brand new
creature and I know nothing at all.'
Then I began to laugh as well.

It was a long journey home, but it did
not seem so very far because my brand new
friend came with me all the way.

Elephant

Snake

Pig

Ostrich

Crocodile

Brand New

Creature

Giraffe

Warthog

Lion